THE
LITTLE
OLD MAN
AND
HIS DREAMS

By Lillian Ross

Paintings by Deborah Healy

Harper & Row, Publishers

The Little Old Man and His Dreams
Text copyright © 1990 by Lillian Hammer Ross
Illustrations copyright © 1990 by Deborah Healy
Printed in the U.S.A. All rights reserved.
Typography by Patricia Tobin
First Edition
10 9 8 7 6 5 4 3 2 1

Library of Congress Cataloging-in-Publication Data
Ross, Lillian.
    The little old man and his dreams / by Lillian Ross ; pictures by
Deborah Healy.
        p.   cm.
    "A Charlotte Zolotow book."
    Summary: God comes to an old man in his dreams and allows him to
attend his granddaughter's wedding; but in return the old man must
come to live with God.
    ISBN 0-06-025094-1 : $. — ISBN 0-06-025095-X (lib. bdg.) : $
    [1. Old age—Fiction.   2. Jews—Fiction.   3. Weddings—Fiction.
4. Dreams—Fiction.]   I. Healy, Deborah, ill.   II. Title.
PZ7.R719696Li 1990   89-34511
[E]—dc20   CIP
                                                                          AC

To my granddaughters Jenna and Emily

Many years ago, when only birds dared to fly, there lived a Little Old Man. Some said he was 90 years old. Some said he was 100 years old. Some said he was, like Moses, 120 years old.

In a village over the mountain lived the Little Old Man's granddaughter, Shoshanna. Her auburn hair fell in ringlets about her face. Her dark eyes sparkled with the joy of life. Her soft, full mouth smiled from inner happiness.

Shoshanna fell in love with a tall and handsome young man. The betrothal was announced and the wedding date set. The Little Old Man was overjoyed that he would see his granddaughter stand beneath the wedding chuppah on the first night of Chanukah. He remembered the day of her birth and the happiness he had felt when she had been blessed with the name Shoshanna. Shoshanna, the rose. Shoshanna, the name of his beloved wife, who had died long ago.

He thought of the little girl running toward him. Where had that little girl gone? He still remembered the nights he had held her, and together they had lit the Chanukah candles. Shoshanna, the child, was to be a married woman.

The Little Old Man made ready his horse and wagon to travel over the mountain. He prepared his prayer book and tallit, his wedding suit, a bottle of wine, a basket of fruit, and a warm blanket. He placed them in the wagon.

In a deep pocket of his coat the Little Old Man hid his dear wife's pearls. The pearls were his special gift for Shoshanna.

The crisp winter day gave hint of a storm, but the Little Old Man felt good to be on his way. The first stop would be at the home of old friends who lived halfway through his journey to Shoshanna's village.

The Little Old Man traveled for two hours when the wagon wheel lodged itself in a mud hole. He looked up at the heavens. "Do troubles never end?" He got out of the wagon and grabbed hold of the wheel. It was too heavy to lift. The Little Old Man took everything out of the wagon. It was still too heavy. He sat by the horse and moaned, "Look at me. I do not have the strength to help myself. Now I will not be at Shoshanna's wedding." He covered his head with his hands and wept.

The horse licked the salty tears. The Little Old Man looked at his horse. "Come," he said. "I am old and you are not so old. I will help you, and you will pull the wagon out of this hole."

He found a gnarled branch and dug around the wheel. When he felt he had cleared enough dirt, the Little Old Man pulled the reins. "Come, my friend. Pull, pull. We must be on our way to Shoshanna's wedding."

But the wagon would not move.

Again the Little Old Man dug, loosening the soil around the wheel. He dropped rocks into the opening that circled the rim and once again pulled the horse's reins. The wagon lifted, then sank back into the hole.

"Old friend, is this as far as we go? At my age, I cannot get myself up on your back and I cannot walk over the mountain. Do we sit and wait for another traveler?"

The Little Old Man leaned against the horse and sighed. After some time, he turned to his horse. "The Lord helps those who help themselves." He dug and pushed the rocks around the wheel, took hold of the reins, and called, "Come, old friend, let's help ourselves." The animal followed the pull of the Little Old Man and suddenly lurched forward to free the captive wheel.

The Little Old Man again placed his prayer book and tallit, his wedding suit, the bottle of wine, the basket of fruit, and his warm blanket in the wagon. He patted his inner pocket that held the precious pearls and climbed onto the wagon. The Little Old Man laughed. "Shoshanna," he called, "we are on our way."

Winter clouds gathered, and the darkness of a threatening storm caused the Little Old Man to urge his horse to trot faster. The rain began slowly, growing into a burst that forced the Little Old Man to crouch beneath his blanket while he held his horse's reins. The wintry storm continued, and he trembled with cold.

Water-soaked, he reached the house of his friends. Exhaustion seeped into his old bones, and he feared that illness would keep him from Shoshanna's wedding. His good friends gave him hot tea and put him into bed with a poultice on his chest and a warming iron at his feet.

But his cold turned to fever, and with the fever came delirium. The Little Old Man tossed on his bed. He coughed and coughed, trying to cough out the illness that possessed his old body. He sensed his friends by the side of the bed, and he heard their prayers for his return to health. For two nights the fever held.

On the third night, the Little Old Man won his battle and slept quietly. He dreamed he walked up the tall mountain that looked down on his small village. He dreamed he went to see the King.

"My most beloved King," began the Little Old Man. "Please, I beg of you, grant me one wish. Please allow me to see my Shoshanna wed."

"If I am to grant your wish, old man," spoke the King, "there are two vows you need pledge to me."

"Yes, yes." The Little Old Man's face shone with joy.

"First, you must trust me."

"Yes, yes," whispered the Little Old Man.

"Second, you must pray, with a full and devoted heart, that your wish be granted."

"I will," promised the Little Old Man, and with the dream's end, he slept quietly.

Two days before Chanukah, the Little Old Man stood with his friends in thankful prayer. He was well enough to travel. Again he placed his prayer book and tallit, his wedding suit and his warm blanket, in the wagon. He felt his inner pocket for his precious gift of pearls, thanked his friends, and was on his way to Shoshanna's wedding.

As the wind grew colder, the Little Old Man wrapped himself in his blanket and urged the horse on. He remembered his dream and his pledge to trust the King. He covered his head with his tallit and prayed for a safe journey. He was deep in prayer and did not see the figures hidden in the branches of an ancient oak. Two men dropped on him.

"Give us your gold!" they shouted.

They threw the Little Old Man from his wagon.

"I have no gold," he cried.

The men pounded on his old body. "Give us your money!" they demanded.

"I have no money," he cried again.

One robber held the old man's arms and the other searched his pockets.

"Pearls. We found your jewels, old man."

"No! They are for my granddaughter." The Little Old Man grabbed for the pearls and held them with all his strength.

"You old fool," yelled the robbers. As they wrenched the pearls away, the chain broke and the pearls scattered on the ground. The robbers scuffled in the dirt, snatched up the pearls, and ran off laughing.

The Little Old Man put his clenched fists around the horse's neck and sobbed. When he felt silence in the winter's cold, the Little Old Man opened his eyes.

"Gone? Have they gone?" he asked the winter sky. "Thanks be to God. I am still alive, and my horse is here to take me to Shoshanna's wedding."

He took his arms from the horse's neck and opened his hands. One pearl rested in the folds of his glove. The Little Old Man sighed. "My dear wife, only one of your pearls will go to our granddaughter, but it carries the beauty and the memories of our long-ago life together."

He folded his tallit, climbed up onto the wagon, and picked up the reins. "Come, my friend, we are going to a wedding." And into the wind, he shouted, "Shoshanna, we are on our way!"

When the Little Old Man arrived at his granddaughter's house, everyone ran to greet him. "Grandfather," said Shoshanna, "we were so worried. Why were you so long in coming?"

"The winter's storm and two ruffians played terrible tricks on your grandfather. Thanks to God, I am here." The Little Old Man smiled at his granddaughter. "Look at you. A woman. A bride."

Shoshanna hugged the Little Old Man. "Oh, Grandfather, I am so happy you are here. We have been waiting for you. You were so late, I was afraid we would have to postpone the wedding."

"Postpone the wedding?" the Little Old Man gasped. "Shoshanna, one does not put off the blessings of a wedding."

Shoshanna smiled, "You are safe and you are here, Grandfather. My wedding and having you with me are a twofold blessing."

In bed for the night, the Little Old Man whispered, "The Lord moves in magnificent ways," and fell asleep. Again he dreamed he climbed the tall mountain. Again he dreamed he went to see the King. He stood before this majestic King and he could not speak.

"You have come to see me again, old man. What would you say to your King?"

No words came from the Little Old Man.

"You have been promised your one wish, old man," said the King. "That one wish was to see your granddaughter wed. You have not as yet received your wish. It is not your time to come with me." The King smiled at the Little Old Man. "It is not your time."

The Little Old Man sat up in bed. Was that a dream? Why dream such a dream? If he could have spoken, what would he have said to the King? The Little Old Man shook his head. "Not my time," he said, and once again fell fast asleep.

It was the first night of Chanukah. As Shoshanna sang the blessings, the first candle of freedom was lit. The ancient rabbis called these Chanukah lights a miracle. The Little Old Man looked at the flickering candlelight. "Is all of life as fragile as a Chanukah flame?" he whispered. "And is it a miracle that I am here?"

He turned toward Shoshanna and her young man as they stood beneath the chuppah. His mind flew back to his youth when he, too, stood with his betrothed beneath the chuppah of her grandfather's tallit. The Little Old Man blinked his eyes. "Today is today," he softly sighed. "A new life is beginning."

Shoshanna's young man raised her veil and offered the blessed wine from their marriage goblet. The rabbi lifted his hands in blessing, and once again the Little Old Man remembered his own wedding canopy and heard the rabbi. "Blessed is the man that hath a virtuous wife, for the number of his days shall be doubled." The Little Old Man smiled. "Shoshanna, you were my good wife," he whispered. "And now our granddaughter becomes a wife."

The rabbi spoke and the young man repeated, "With this ring you are wedded to me, in accordance with the laws of Moses and of Israel."

"Mazel tov!" called everyone as the bridegroom stomped on the glass wrapped in its white cloth. He gathered the bride in his arms. Around Shoshanna's neck one small pearl gleamed on a pink ribbon.

The fiddlers began, and friends showered the bride and groom with wheat and coins. "Be fruitful and multiply," they sang. The children scurried about gathering up the coins, and once again the Little Old Man felt the excitement of his own wedding, seated by his bride. With the magic of the music, he danced the memory of his wedding joy, his own Shoshanna in his arms. Around her neck the strand of perfect pearls reflected the happiness that glowed upon her cheeks.

"Grandfather, come dance with me," his granddaughter said softly.

The Little Old Man shook himself awake. "Shoshanna, I have been remembering my own wedding. How your blessed grandmother and I danced in that long-ago time."

"So dance with me now, Grandfather," Shoshanna coaxed, and the Little Old Man held this dear Shoshanna in his arms.

That night, when the Little Old Man went to bed, his head was full of music and his arms tingled with happiness. The dancing and the wine and the joy of the wedding eased him into sleep. Once again he dreamed he returned to the palace of the great King. He dreamed he walked up to this most regal King.

"Speak, old man," the King commanded. "This is your time to speak."

"My dear beloved King," said the Little Old Man, "now I have the words to thank you for the gift of Shoshanna's wedding."

"You trusted me"—smiled the King—"as I trust you."

And in his dreams this great King took him by the hand, and the Little Old Man lived forevermore in the palace of the noble King with his beloved wife, his own Shoshanna.